SUNGWAN SO is a freelance photographer specialising in travel and documentary photography. Born in Hong Kong, he has a degree in Anthropology and a Masters in Philosophy from the Chinese University of Hong Kong, where he majored in peasant economy, social changes and minorities issues in China. He went on to study photography at the Brooks Institute of Photography in California, and now lives in the USA. *C is for China* is his first book.

To my dear parents So Hing Bun and Ho Sook Chun,
my lovely wife Mabel Leung and my friends in China,
especially Li Yifu and his family – S.S.

C is for China copyright © Frances Lincoln Limited 1997
Text and photographs copyright © Sungwan So 1997

First published in Great Britain in 1997 by
Frances Lincoln Limited, 4 Torriano Mews
Torriano Avenue, London NW5 2RZ

First paperback edition 1998

British Library Cataloguing in Publication Data
available on request

ISBN 0-7112-1318-6

Set in 15/20pt Palatino
Printed in Hong Kong

1 3 5 7 9 8 6 4 2

The publishers would like to acknowledge
Mabel Leung as co-writer of the text.

C is for CHINA

Sungwan So

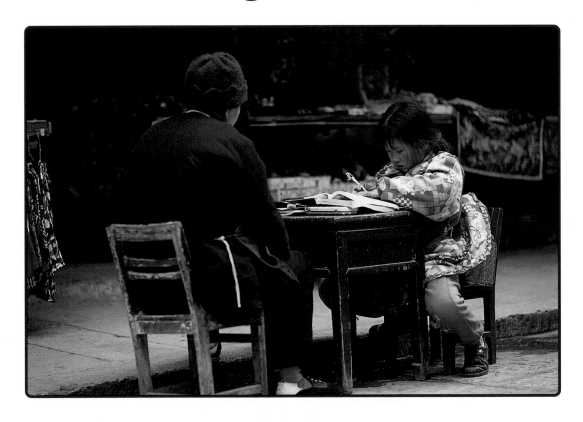

FRANCES LINCOLN

Author's note

China is one of the largest countries in the world, almost as big as the whole of Europe, and one quarter of the world's population is Chinese. Modern China has developed from an ancient civilisation and features of Ancient China are evident in today's art, architecture and society.

My family come from Guangdong province in southern China. These photographs were taken there, as well as in Guangxi, Yunnan and Shanxi. It is impossible to show the entire breadth of this vast country, but I have tried to illustrate the common beliefs held by Chinese people and some of their customs, both ancient and modern: their commitment to hard work, their strong sense of family, history and religion, and their optimism about the future. Images of cities and the countryside show the rich diversity of lifestyles and landscapes, but these are just a taste of what China has to offer. I hope this book will inspire you to visit and explore our country – you are welcome any time!

算盤

Aa

is for Abacus, a calculating frame with beads which slide on thin rods. The top two beads each equal 5, and the lower five each equal 1. Even though electronic calculators are becoming popular, many people still prefer to use an abacus – it can be just as fast.

自行车

Bb is for Bicycle, the most common way to travel. China has been called 'The Kingdom of Bicycles' because, whatever the weather, we cycle to school and to work, to the market and shops, and from one village to another. As we cycle through crowds and traffic, we ring our bicycle bells to warn pedestrians, other cyclists and drivers that we are coming.

Cc is for China, one of the largest countries in the world. Riverboats are used to transport people and carry goods across the country. The longest rivers are Yellow River and Yangtze River which flow for thousands of kilometres from west to east, and Li River is renowned for its stunning beauty.

中国

Dd is for Dragon, a legendary animal which is a symbol of strength and luck. With antelope horns, a snake-like body covered in fish scales and bird-shaped feet, dragons were said to fly through the sky and swim across oceans. The symbol of the dragon is often found in palaces, temples and as decoration in people's homes.

龙

煅
鍊

 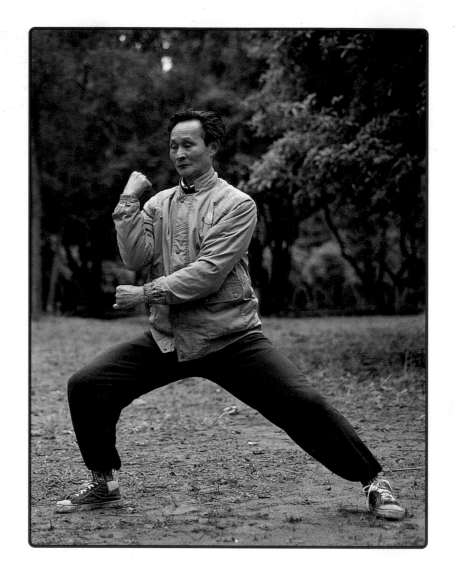

Ee is for Exercise. Chinese people practise a body exercise called Tai Ji. It is a sequence of very slow, circular movements and controlled breathing. Tai Ji is practised in the early morning, in outdoor spaces.

Ff

is for Fengzheng, a Chinese kite. Fengzheng flying is popular and we like to make our own with paper and string. The shapes of a butterfly or bird are common, although sometimes fengzheng are shaped like dragons, caterpillars and other creatures.

风筝

花园

Gg

is for Garden. Many gardens
which were owned by wealthy
families hundreds of years ago
are public parks today. Pagodas,
ornamental structures shaped
like temples, were built in the
parks, and words describing the
beautiful scenery are inscribed
on them.

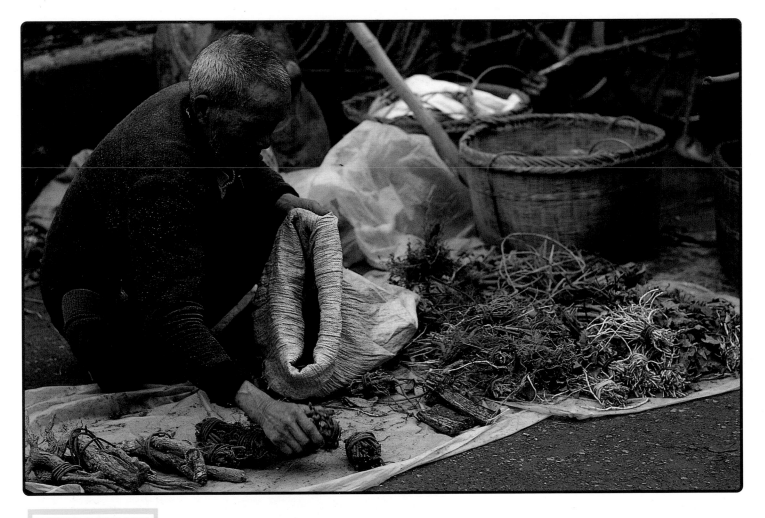

草药

Hh

is for Herbal medicine, made from the roots, stems and leaves of plants. According to ancient legends, Shennong, the God of Farmers, tasted all kinds of plants and recorded the medicinal use of them. For many years these plants were gathered from the mountains, but nowadays people grow them. They are then sold in markets, or in traditional herbal medicine shops.

Ii

is for Incense, a mixture of aromatic spices burnt as an offering to gods, heroes and ancestors, either at home or in a temple. On the birthday of Confucius, the ancient Chinese philosopher, teachers bring children to his temple, where they light a fire and burn joss sticks and paper money as an offering.

is for Jade, a precious stone which can be different shades of green, yellow or red. It is cut and shaped into bracelets or pendants which are worn from an early age, as we believe that jade protects us from evil spirits.

厨房

Kk is for Kitchen. There is a Chinese proverb, "Food comes first among all things," and the kitchen is the focal point of each home. Although electrical appliances like rice cookers are common, we still use traditional utensils: a big, flat knife for chopping and a wok to stir-fry vegetables, meat and fish.

Ll

灯笼

is for Lantern, the traditional lamp in China. It is made of thin paper which wraps around a bamboo frame supporting a candle inside. Nowadays electric bulbs have replaced candles. Large, red lanterns are hung outside palaces or temples as decoration. They are also hung at the front doors of houses during times of celebration, such as weddings, birthdays or Chinese New Year.

市场

Mm

is for Market. In parts of China, peasants are self-sufficient – they grow and produce their own food. They sell some of their crops and vegetables in the market in order to buy things that they cannot grow or make, like chemical fertiliser.

Nn

面条

is for Noodles, a typical dish eaten plain or with other food. Noodles are made from wheat, rice or corn, and are fried or served in soup. We eat them with chopsticks. Some stories say the explorer, Marco Polo, brought noodles from China to Italy, where they became spaghetti.

Oo is for Old. There is a Chinese proverb saying, "Old folk in your family are your treasure." We believe that the elderly have knowledge and experience from which the young can benefit, and we greatly respect them.

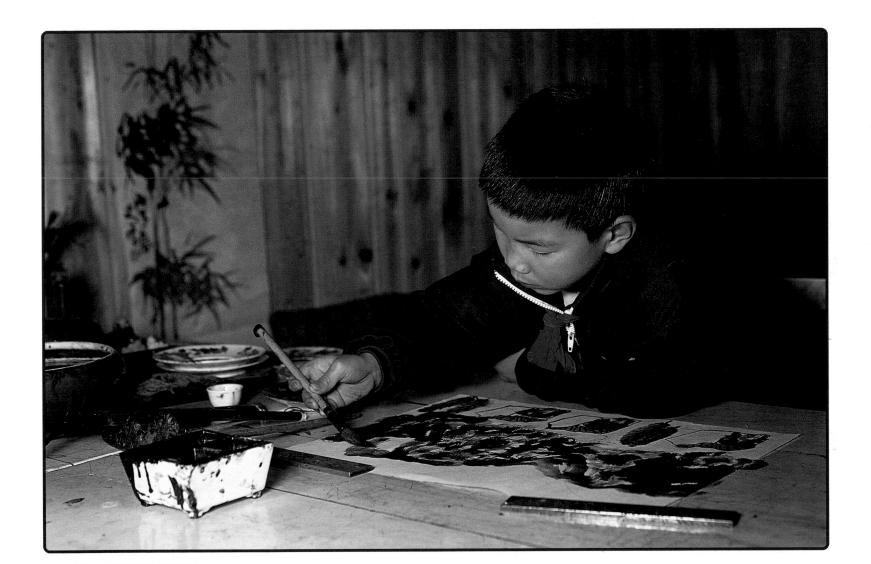

P p is for Picture, drawn in ink-and-wash or *shuimohua*. Different shades of black are created using water. The more water added, the lighter shade of black. Colour is added to the picture only as a final touch or highlight.

清明

Qq

is for Qingming Festival, the day when we pay tribute to our ancestors. Schoolchildren throw flowers at monuments, erected as a reminder of the Communist Revolution and as a sign of respect to past leaders and heroes who sacrificed their lives for the Revolution.

人民币

Rr

is for Renminbi, the Chinese currency. Each note, apart from the 100-yuan note, shows the faces of farmers and factory workers, and people from different ethnic groups, to symbolise the union of a country made up of a variety of cultures.

唱歌

Ss

is for Singing. Not everybody can read and write in rural China, so they express their feelings, or even pass knowledge on to the next generation, through songs. Some people sing love songs to each other through bamboo 'telephones'. These are made from two hollow pieces of bamboo joined with string. Sound vibrations from the singing travel along the string.

跳棋

 Tt is for Tiaoqi, a type of chess game using different coloured marbles. Each player has ten marbles and the aim of the game is to move them to the opposite corner of the board by jumping across other marbles. The game can be played with up to six people.

Uu

is for Uniform, worn by the police. It is green in summer and brown in winter. On the left sleeve is a red star that represents China, and an emblem of the Great Wall which symbolises the protection offered by the police. They also wear caps and belts, and large snow jackets in winter.

制服

蔬菜

 Vv is for Vegetables, an important part of our diet. After the harvest, vegetables are dried in the sun, a cheap way of preserving them. The sun-dried vegetables provide food during the harsh winter months.

文字

Ww

is for Wenzi or Chinese writing.
We use characters, developed from
pictures, each with its own meaning.
We read them from top to bottom
and from right to left. Traditional
Chinese writing is considered an art.

Xx is for Xiao, a musical instrument from ancient times. It is made from a piece of hollow bamboo and is played like a recorder, by blowing through a hole at the top. The player's fingers cover different holes along the length of the bamboo to produce different sounds.

Yy is for Yellow, a colour that in the past was worn and used only by the royal family. Today yellow is a colour for everyone. Schoolchildren wear yellow safety caps so that they can be easily seen on the streets.

禅

Zz

is for Zen, a major religion
(commonly known as Chan)
which developed from Buddhism.
It teaches inner peace through
meditation and enlightenment.
The Zen monks shave their hair
to symbolize the removal of all
the worries of the world.
They pray every day, counting
their prayers as beads on the
Zen necklace.

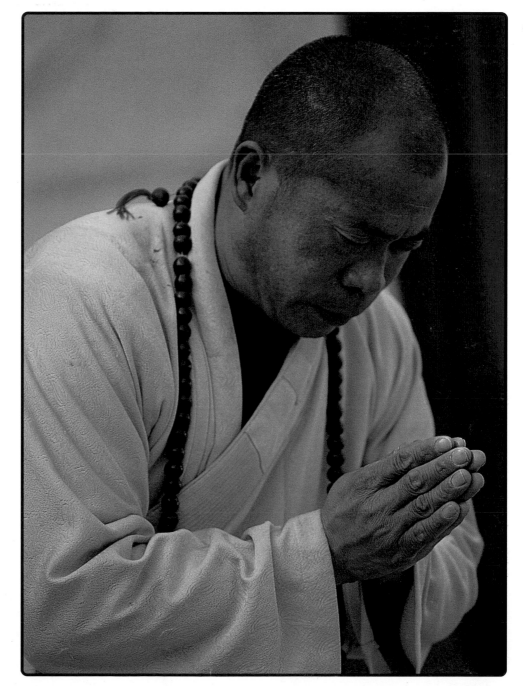